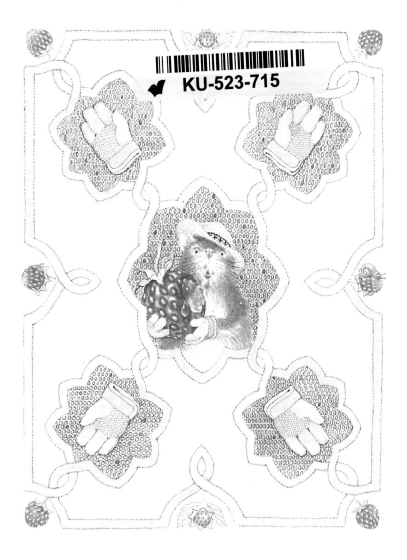

First published 1986 by
Walker Books Ltd
184-192 Drummond Street
London NW1 3HP

Text © 1986 Judy Taylor
Illustrations © 1986 Peter Cross

First printed 1986
Reprinted 1986
Printed and bound by L.E.G.O., Vicenza, Italy

British Library Cataloguing in Publication Data
Cross, Peter
Dudley and the strawberry shake. – (Dudley the dormouse;3)
I. Title   II. Taylor, Judy   III. Series
823'.914[J]   PZ7

ISBN 0-7445-0459-7

DUDLEY
AND THE
STRAWBERRY SHAKE

PETER CROSS
Text by
JUDY TAYLOR

WALKER BOOKS
LONDON

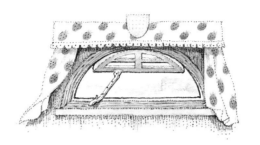

There was a soft breeze
blowing in Shadyhanger and it
carried the scent of strawberries
through the open window.

Dudley had been awake
since early morning searching
for his special gloves.
Today he was going
strawberry picking.

The sun was shining strongly
and the ground felt warm.

Dudley set off with his
berry-barrow down the lane
to the strawberry patch, and
long before he got there
his mouth was watering.

As he turned the corner,
there they were before him –
row upon row of fat, juicy
strawberries.

BEWARE
OF THE
DOG.

Dudley picked a
big strawberry very
carefully with his
special gloves.

He took a bite
to see if it was ripe.
It was.

He took another
bite just to make
sure… and another
and another…

until there was
nothing left.
Dudley was quite
full up.

Just then, over by the hedge,
Dudley spied an extra large
strawberry, the largest
he had ever seen.

'That's the one I'll take
home for lunch,' he said.

Dudley gripped the strawberry
firmly with his gloves but
it wouldn't come.

He tried again, pulling
and pulling with all
his might.

Suddenly the strawberry
began to shake
violently.

Dudley hung
on until he felt his
hands slipping out
of his gloves.

Then he was sailing
through the air. He landed
on the grass with a BUMP.

'What an odd strawberry,'
thought Dudley, feeling
rather giddy.

Dudley waited until the world had stopped going round.

'It feels like time for a nap,' he said, hurrying home.

And just as he was drifting off to sleep, Dudley remembered he had left his gloves behind.